Presented To

....

From

....

Date

....

BETHANY BACKYARD®

www.bethanyhouse.com

To Brittany Lynn Bosca,

with love from Aunt Elspeth.

Happy Easter, God!
Text © 2001 by Elspeth Campbell Murphy
Illustrations © 2001 by Bethany House Publishers
Design and production by Lookout Design Group, Inc. (www.lookoutdesign.com)

Scripture quotations identified NIV are from the HOLY BIBLE, NEW INTERNATIONAL VERSION®. Copyright © 1973, 1978, 1984 by International Bible Society. Used by permission of Zondervan Publishing House. All rights reserved. The "NIV" and "New International Version" trademarks are registered in the United States Patent and Trademark Office by International Bible Society. Use of either trademark requires the permission of International Bible Society.

Scripture quotations identified ICB are from the *International Children's Bible, New Century Version*, copyright © 1986, 1988 by Word Publishing, Dallas, Texas 75039. Used by permission.

Scripture quotations identified TEV are from the Bible in Today's English Version *Good News Bible*. Copyright © American Bible Society 1966, 1971, 1976, 1992.

Published by Bethany House Publishers
A Ministry of Bethany Fellowship International
11400 Hampshire Avenue South
Bloomington, Minnesota 55438
www.bethanyhouse.com

Printed in China.

Library of Congress Cataloging-in-Publication data applied for.

Dear Grown-up,

The young child's response to the world is up close and personal. And something happens for us when we look at God's world through a young child's imaginative eyes: Our own faith is freshened.

That's why the Scripture verses are included in this book— for your own meditation. For example, in one prayer-poem the child delights in holding a rabbit. And the accompanying verse (Deuteronomy 33:27a) reminds us, as adults, that *we* are supported by the everlasting arms.

So share this book and God's world with your young child. And may God richly bless you both!

Elspeth Campbell Murphy

Good Morning!

Today I saw the sun come up!

Hooray!

It's Easter morning!

> Good morning, sun.
> Good morning, sky.
> Good morning, robin hopping by.
> Good morning, grass.
> Good morning, trees.
> Good morning, flowery Easter
> breeze.
> Good morning, God—

You made this day.

Hooray!

It's Easter morning!

Basket Rabbit

First I nibbled his ears.
Then I munched on his nose.
I bit off his tail.
And gobbled his toes.

You know why the rabbit didn't mind?

He's the chocolate kind.

Then they took him down from the cross and laid him in a tomb. But God raised him up from death! After this, for many days, the people who had gone with Jesus from Galilee to Jerusalem saw him. They are now his witnesses to the people.

ACTS 13:29b–31 (ICB)

Easter Greeting

You hand me the prettiest egg you can see.
"Christ is risen,"
You say to me.

I reach in the basket and find you one, too.
"He is risen indeed,"
I say to you.

Nothing in all creation is

hidden from God's sight.

HEBREWS 4:13a (NIV)

Easter Egg Hunt

Ha!" said the Easter egg.
"You can't find *me!*"
I told the Easter egg,
"Wait and see."

"Nope!" said the egg.
"You can search high and low,
But you won't find—
Whoops!
Well, what do you know!"

Praise him with trumpets.

PSALM 150:3a (TEV)

Easter Lily

The Easter lily
　　stands quietly,
　　making no sound
　　as it looks around.

But the Easter lily
　　so soft
　　so white

looks like a trumpet,
and I think it might
want to *be* a trumpet.

The blooms burst open as if to say
　　Ta-Daa!
　　TA-DAA!
　　It's EASTER today!

To Church on
Easter Morning

Oh, I'm bouncing along in my Easter bonnet
My Easter bonnet
My Easter bonnet
I'm bouncing along in my Easter bonnet
To church on Easter morning.

Oh, I'm twirling along in my Easter dress
My Easter dress
My Easter dress
I'm twirling along in my Easter dress
To church on Easter morning.

Oh, I'm skipping along in my Easter shoes
My Easter shoes
My Easter shoes
I'm skipping along in my Easter shoes
To church on Easter morning.
To church on Easter morning!

To church on Easter morning!

Then the people brought their

little children to Jesus so that

he could put his hands on

them and pray for them….

Jesus said, "Let the little

children come to me."

MATTHEW 19:13–14a(ICB)

Welcome!

Welcome!
Welcome!
How do you do?"

"I'm just fine, thanks.
How are you?"

"Very well,
I'm pleased to say."

"Glad to hear it!
Lovely day."

"Yes, it is!
Please come on in.
Welcome!
Welcome!

Welcome again!"

Sleepy Bunny

Soft, snuggly bunny,
   hush-a-bye.

Sweet, sleepy bunny,
   close your eyes.

For I know how to hold you—
   gently
   gently.

I know how to talk to you—
   quietly
   quietly.

With a twitch of your nose

And a flick of your ear.

Go to sleep, little bunny.
   I'm here.

A Story! A Story!

A story!
A story!
Read me a story!
Read me a story and let me look
At all the pictures in the book.

Open it!
Open it!
Open it wide!
Open the book—
There's a *story* inside!

Jerusalem

Come with me to Jerusalem
   To Jerusalem
   Oh, Jerusalem!
Let us go up to Jerusalem
And see what we shall see.

For Jesus is there in Jerusalem
   The Son of God
   In Jerusalem.
Let us hear him tell of the love of God—
God's love for you and me.

And the cross is there in Jerusalem
   Where Jesus died
   In Jerusalem.
The saddest day of all sad days
The world will ever see.

But come with me to the empty tomb
   In Jerusalem
   Oh, Jerusalem!
For our risen Lord is alive this day
And calls to you and me.

The Lord takes care of his people

    like a shepherd.

He gathers the people like lambs

    in his arms.

He carries them close to him.

Paper Lamb

Paper, cotton balls, and glue,
Little Lamb, I'm making *you!*

In a little while you'll be
Standing right in front of me.

It's a happy thing, they say,
To meet a lamb on Easter day.

Lord, you have made so many things!

How wisely you made them all!

The earth is filled with your creatures.

PSALM 104:24 (TEV)

Armful of Ducklings

Oh, I wish I could scoop up an armful of ducklings;

I wish I could fill all my pockets with ducklings—

God's

Dear

Little

Darling

Adorable

Ducklings—

Oh, Ducklings!

I wish I could carry you home!

Butterfly

God's buttery yellow butterfly
Fluttered by
Fluttered by
Looking for a place to rest.

I felt a tickle on my wrist,
A tiny tickle on my wrist,
And I looked up to see
That of all the places in the yard
The butterfly
Picked ME!

After this I heard what

sounded like a great many

people in heaven. They

were saying: "Hallelujah!

[Praise the Lord.]

Salvation, glory, and power

belong to our God."

REVELATION 19:1 (ICB)

Shout Hallelujah!

Shout, "Hallelujah!"
And cry, "Happy Easter!"
For Jesus has risen,
Our Lord and our Friend.

Shout "Hallelujah!"
For we are God's children.
We will celebrate Easter
FOREVER!
Amen!

Dear friends, now we are children of God. We have not yet been

shown what we will be in the future. But we know when Christ

comes again, we will be like him. We will see him as he really is.

1 JOHN 3:2 (ICB)